Abdul

Dial Books for Young Readers
New York

Abdul

by Rosemary Wells

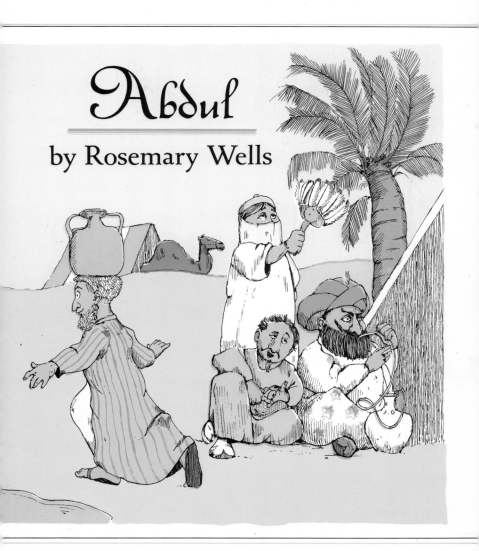

Dial Books for Young Readers
A Division of E. P. Dutton
A Division of New American Library
2 Park Avenue, New York, New York 10016

Published simultaneously in Canada
by Fitzhenry & Whiteside Limited, Toronto

Library of Congress Catalog Card Number: 74-18595

Printed in Hong Kong
by South China Printing Co.
First Pied Piper Printing 1986
COBE
10 9 8 7 6 5 4 3 2 1

A Pied Piper Book is a registered trademark of
Dial Books for Young Readers, a division of E. P. Dutton,
a division of New American Library, ® TM 1,163,686 and ® TM 1,054,312

ABDUL
is published in a hardcover edition by Dial Books for Young Readers.
ISBN 0-8037-0281-7

The art for this book was prepared in four colors, using a base
black-line pen-and-ink drawing with from 3 to 7 Bourges and Transparent
Red Masking Medium acetate overlays for each spread.

For my husband, Farouk

Feisal and his old mother camel, Gilda,
lived on an oasis in the middle of the desert.

Every summer Gilda had three lovely children.
Everyone came to admire them, even Sheik Gamaliel.

But one summer Gilda had only a single
baby. What a terrible-looking camel!
she thought, and she hid him. Unfortunately
the oasis dried up that very day.

"My Gilda has a little surprise for Papa?" said Feisal.

He pulled young Abdul out by the tail.

"Gilda, my angel!" said Feisal. "What have you done to me? This camel is a disaster! Where is his hump? Look at his toes! With those feet he will never cross the desert, and we are leaving in half an hour!"

Gilda would not leave without Abdul,

so Feisal had to rig a special device to carry him.

Luckily it was so hot nobody noticed.

But days passed, and the camels began
to droop. Everyone got thirstier
and thirstier.

Soon people started grumbling about
their bad luck.

One night Omar, the machete sharpener, said,
"Look at that ugly creature in Feisal's saddlebag!
It has a face like an axe!"
"It wouldn't surprise me one bit," said Omar's
wife Fatima, "if it was some kind of devil!"

"Devil?" asked Ben Berber.
"Did someone say devil?"

The word soon spread to Sheik Gamaliel.

"Devil!" said Sheik Gamaliel. "Is it any wonder that Mother Desert gives us nothing to drink?

Seize him and tie him to
a stake and we'll leave
him here to starve."

But Gilda would not budge without Abdul

so all three were left behind.

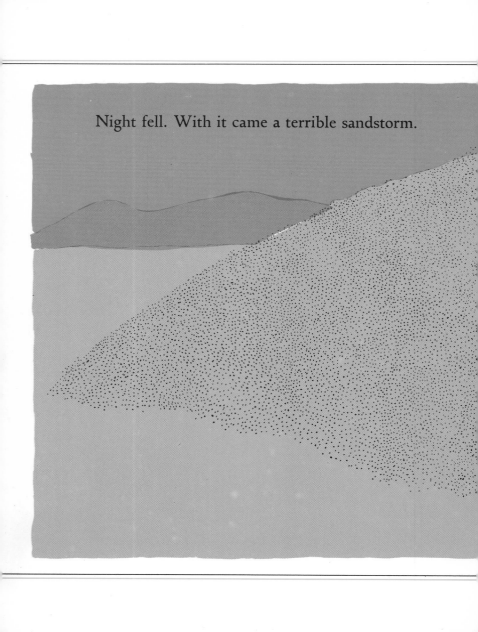

Night fell. With it came a terrible sandstorm.

In the morning Abdul was nowhere in sight.
"Allah be praised," said Feisal. "Now we
must catch up with the others."

But Gilda wanted to find Abdul.

After many hours she discovered him
at a nice new oasis.

Among new friends.

None of Abdul's new friends
had ever seen a horse as
funny-looking as Gilda.

But Gilda wouldn't leave without
Abdul so they had to stay on.